Ajji And Other Stories

NYC Big Book Award
2019 Distinguished Favourite

VINODA REVANNASIDDAIAH

BLUEROSE PUBLISHERS

India | U.K.

Copyright © Vinoda Revannasiddaiah 2023

All rights reserved by author. No part of this publication may be reproduced, stored in a retrieval system or transmitted in any form or by any means, electronic, mechanical, photocopying, recording or otherwise, without the prior permission of the author. Although every precaution has been taken to verify the accuracy of the information contained herein, the publisher assumes no responsibility for any errors or omissions. No liability is assumed for damages that may result from the use of information contained within.

BlueRose Publishers takes no responsibility for any damages, losses, or liabilities that may arise from the use or misuse of the information, products, or services provided in this publication.

For permissions requests or inquiries regarding this publication, please contact:

BLUEROSE PUBLISHERS
www.BlueRoseONE.com
info@bluerosepublishers.com
+91 8882 898 898
+4407342408967

ISBN: 978-93-5819-761-7

Cover Painting: Vinoda Revannasiddaiah

First Edition: December 2023

For my husband and children who are my constant support.

CONTENTS

AJJI	1
THERE WAS LIFE IN STONE	10
BLOOD CANNOT LIE	22
GIVING UP	32
RANGI	39
RINA'S DOLLS	51
SELF DIGNITY	62
A NEST IN WINTER	71
PARVATI	80
THE CRYSTAL BALL	91
CHANDRIKA	98
ABOUT THE AUTHOR	110

AJJI

Seventy-four years stretched between my great-grandmother and me, she being 84 and I, 10, and yet there seemed to be no distance in years at all. She was as helpless and sensitive as a child, bursting into tears very often, and in all my experience, these tears were what I understood best. She loved playing dice just as I did. Six pieces of dice, a piece of chalk and cowries were all that we needed to get started. I drew the chart on the floor and then we cast the dice like the future rolled out of our hands. But Ajji invariably cheated. She kept me engrossed in her stories while she stealthily turned the dice in her palm
,feeling the numbers before she cast the dice for a high score. 'Don't cheat, Ajji,' I shouted when I caught her and she retorted, 'Once in a while, my child, it's alright. It's a game, after

all. She laughed like a child too, her face reddening and her great big stomach rolling like a rock down a mountain. Her chin had sharp hair, like bristles on a gourd. I felt snug and warm, resting against her soft pillow-like arm and my little palm in hers must have comforted her. I loved to sleep on her huge lap, listening to the same stories over and over again, waiting for her to confuse names and facts so that I could pounce on her mistakes with fiery pleasure.

'Vinu, come, let us go for a walk,' she would call and I knew that what it really meant was : *take me for a walk.* I helped her push her feet into her *chappals* and held her arm. She walked slowly and unsurely, afraid of the little pebbles that might upset her balance. And then we would talk of long ago, as we sat beneath the mango trees . . .

My great-grandmother--my Ajji--belonged to that fortunate group from India's glorious past, whose lifestyle is, today, an incredible fairy tale. Her husband had won the high honour of 'Rao Bahaddur', bestowed on him by the Maharaja of Mysore. He had parted with enormous wealth to establish a free 'Choultry' for poor students who aspired for education. Like him, Ajji also showered immeasurable munificence on the poor and so, she and her husband were esteemed as the honoured guardians of society. Nobility and charity were inborn to them. She loved to talk about herself and shut her eyes like a cat when she mused about her bygone days.

'When I was a bride, they spoke of me as a Lakshmi who had come home and they took me in through the back door.'

'Why the back door, Ajji?' I asked.

'Because I was my husband's third wife and the most beautiful. The others bore no children, the two elder wives. I was chosen only after the fortune-tellers promised I would bear a son.'

That son was my maternal grandfather who took a second wife after the death of his first, who had left behind my mother and my uncle whom we called 'Mama.'

'I never gave them up to the care of their stepmother,' she repeatedly emphasised. 'I brought up the two motherless children.'

She loved to reminiscence about the riches of her days. 'We had sieves to sort out gems and pearls of different sizes,' she said and I was enchanted by the description.

'When I opened the iron safes, gems poured out and I never cared to pick them up'.

'And who did, Ajji?' 'The servants, of course.'

'And then when it was the season to make brinjal palya, your great- grandfather specially sent a man to Madras to buy them. Bangalore brinjals were not worth it . . . and I supervised the masala myself. Those were the days of ghee and butter and the whole street would smell of my brinjal palya.'

I knew it was true for, once, Mother had allowed Ajji to prepare brinjal palya, using her choicest ingredients and, truly, the whole house was filled with its aroma. I had run to the gate to see if the smell had reached there too and I was thrilled to find passers by turning their faces towards our house. But Mother bitterly complained about the ruthless sweep of ingredients from her store and the 'over and above' expenditure. 'She had better forget her days of splendour,' she sighed, wondering at the thoughtlessness of her extravagance. 'And then we had saris designed with real gold thread, weighing a *maund* !

I so much want to see you in a sari Vinu, why don't you wear one?'

This usually led to a quarrel between us and stretched the distance between

us.

'Well, Ajji, perhaps you should try on a frock as well,' I said. 'I'd so love

to see you in one.'

And both of us would laugh with the glee of little children. Imagine great- grandma in a frock, her huge knees and elbows showing and her fat body looking like a dolled-up ball! I don't know how she pictured herself but, anyway, we laughed together and the distance vanished again.

She was my companion for one month every year when she came to be with us during our summer holidays. She spent the rest of the year in my Mama's house. She had fallen out with her son, my grandfather, who continued the rich life and noble traditions of his family.

'But I will never return to him,' she said,' he has dishonoured me with base words in his wife's presence.' And so, it was my uncle to whom she turned, with pride and trust. When she left us to return to him after our summer holidays, the emptiness belonged not only to her room but more to my little heart. I wept for days after she left.

Then, there came the day when she suffered a shock and her tears would not end when my little hand felt lost in her great, trembling hand. She had come to us again during our holidays and the mango season had just begun. It was her habit to sit outside on the *pial* every afternoon, waiting with closed eyes for the sound of a falling mango. And when she did, she shook herself awake and shouted out to me to run for the fallen mango.

'Mangoes ripened on the tree are the tastiest,'she would say, relishing every bit of the fruit. And it was during this happy season that the sad news came. My uncle had written that he 'had had enough of the responsibility of caring for her and so, did not wish her to return to his home again.' The rudeness of the letter pierced my heart.

'Don't worry, Ajji, stay with us,' I said, but she only sobbed, saying, 'How can I be a burden to a daughter of the family? It's not right.' Mother asked her to stay and father did too, but she refused and decided to 'try again' at her grandson's house. She was helpless and homeless. She cried like a child and I cried with her. I could not understand her terrible sacrifice for the sake of a principle--the mere belief that she should not be a burden to a daughter of the family. She packed her things again, this time, taking care not to leave anything behind and not refusing anything my mother offered, for, who could say what use even the smallest thing would be to her? We rolled her mattress in her striped carpet and tied the rope around it. She folded her own saris as she always did for she would not suffer 'defilement'. The night before she left, I sat for a long time beside her, waiting to see her fall asleep but she would not.

'Vinu . . . when will I see you again, my dear? You married . . . and in a sari . . .' This time neither of us laughed. There were too many tears. She left by train the next day.

Uncle wrote to say that it was indeed unworthy of Mother to have sent Ajji back when he had asked her not to and since keeping her with him was out of the question, he had sent her back to his father, her son. The news greatly upset Mother, for Ajji had vowed never to seek shelter in my grand-father's home. This was great humiliation indeed. It was too late in the day to ask Ajji to undo her decisions. Separated from her by over 482 kilometres, my heart bled for this grand old lady, helpless and humiliated.

The end came when cancer struck. She had always prided herself on her impeccable health. Perhaps only this deadly disease was strong enough to take her away. I had a secret feeling that cancer was only an excuse-- death came because of her own decision to die. It was, in a way, dignified suicide.

She cried for food to satisfy the fire in her stomach and was repeatedly admonished by my step-grandmother for her devilish appetite. She, who had been the hope and solace of countless people, was now a beggar pleading for kindness. My grandfather's Mysore turban, his great black coat and *jari* dhoti together with his image as a 'saviour', and a noble apostle of society; my Mama's popularity as a 'successful businessman' thriving on loads of wealth, were all bitter proof of hypocrisy. She suffered for over two months before she entered a coma and was shifted to the hospital.

We were beside her during her last days. Her eyes were closed and my little palm was no longer felt by her great, big palm. My heart was filled with fear and anguish as I watched the rise and fall of her stomach telling me there was life yet, perhaps signifying the struggle of passage to a painless world.

On that last day, I let in a few spoons of milk through her open mouth. The milk did not flow out. She had swallowed it. That was her silent response to my violent heartbeat; that was her silent good-bye to me, her little friend.

THERE WAS LIFE IN STONE

SLOWLY, Slowly, time squeezed out. Sunil sat at his table, his hands clenched together, staring at nothing, thinking . . . lost in a sense of hopelessness.

He had arrived at Yellapura just a short while ago. The village bus which had brought him had snorted its way through the dust. His head felt giddy with the stench of the villagers around and the smoke of the beedies had almost choked him. He had succumbed to a continuous bout of irritated cough. The villagers had turned around noticing his presence, surveying him from head to toe, inquisitively, sometimes contemptuously. They had stopped the incessant chewing of *paan* to spurt out the word, 'Daaktar' to the unin- formed co-passengers. Sweat had broken out on Sunil's forehead. He had felt like a man in a cage filled with strange animals. The bus had stopped every time there was a passenger on the roadside, waving arms to be picked up. The journey had been exhausting and seemed never-ending.

At last, at one stop the bus had jolted to a dragging halt. The conductor clapped the sides of the bus and the driver stretched his hands behind his head before he descended with a yawn. Baskets and bags were hurled down from the top of the bus.

Looking around, Sunil had asked one of the passengers, 'Is this Yellapura?' 'Huh, huh, Yellapura, can't you see?' the villager had shouted. Carrying his

suitcases, Sunil had coughed his way down the steps.

People had gathered around the pushcart man selling salted puffed rice. They turned around to look at him and their fixed glares had made him

uncomfortable. He had felt like speaking, like explaining his presence and had hurriedly stammered, 'The Government Dispensary, please, could you tell me where it is?'

Immediately he had felt like a fool. The dispensary was right opposite the bus stop, hardly a few feet away. The little urchins had giggled with their hands cupped over their mouths. Sunil was ruffled and ashamed.

A whole crowd of children and adults, laughing and jeering, had followed him to the door of the dispensary. He had knocked and after a loud jarring noise, the bolt was drawn aside. The man who had opened the door was obviously the dispensary chemist. He looked like he had been disturbed from sleep. His hair was unkempt and his face unwashed. He shook himself awake and forcing his eyes wide open, said , 'New Doctor, Sir?'

Sunil had been irritated at his loud voice. 'Please come in. How was the journey, Sir? You must relax. I'll make some coffee.'

Dirty cushions flaunted the metal chairs in the room. Sunil had removed the cushions from one of them before sitting down. He had keenly surveyed the two wooden stands stacked with dusty medicine bottles and the unopened boxes stacked on the floor.

'When did the other Doctor leave?' 'A fortnight ago, Sir.'

'Any patients since?'

'Patients, Sir,' the chemist had laughed, 'don't worry about patients yet.

You need a hot cup of coffee first. I then cook a snack for you.' The chemist had a little kitchen corner in the dispensary itself.

'This is how it used to be when the earlier Doctor was here,' he had murmured, 'I did the cooking for him and he paid me. Nice man, Sir, he paid quite an amount. I was able to send a lot home'.

'What about the patients?' Sunil had persisted, 'How many are there everyday?

'Oh sir, the patients belong to the quacks and to the Goddess Yellamma.' 'What do you mean?'

'They don't trust us, and our medicine, Sir. The previous Doctor left because there was no hope . . .'

'The small pox here was terrible, they say.'

'Terrible sir, and yet the villagers did not allow us to tamper with Amma.' Sunil had gulped his coffee with difficulty.

That evening, he and Rajan, the compounder walked along the roads of Yellapura. In the far distance Sunil could see the solitary temple of Yellamma situated on a hilltop. He could hear the ringing of the temple bells and the loud refrain, 'Udhoh, Udh . . . Oh . . . oh'.

The evening puja at the temple had drawn most of the people from their homes. Sunil felt a strange fear at the immensity of faith that prevailed. The steps were steep and tedious. He heard a little boy tell his sister, 'It will be difficult sister, let us not go'.

'I must Munna', the young lady insisted, 'I must go to Yellamma tonight'.

Her steps were slow and heavy and Sunil could guess she was fast advancing towards childbirth.

'Sister, you will be tired,' the boy was pleading but she would not listen. Sunil decided to follow them, slowly. The plight of the young mother-to-be disturbed him. Could he prevail upon her to stay behind? Rajan warned him against speaking to a woman.

'Never to a lady and never when her mind is set on Yellamma,' he said.

Sunil felt that the young woman's efforts were ridiculous.

At the temple, the crows thronged with their offerings. Countless coconuts were broken and Sunil could hear the loud promise of severe rigours to invoke divine blessings.

'Cure me of my illness, Amma, I will climb to your temple everyday for 40 days!' he heard one feverish voice say.

One of the village quacks was applying 'sacred' paste on a child in the name of Yellamma in order to cure a wound.

'Wow! It is some penicillin that the child needs and here is that fool dabbing her with some blessed paste,' he screamed.

Sunil was stifled by the superstitious beliefs and ignorance of the people. He saw one of the temple priests beating a child with neem leaves. . . the child was said to be possessed by evil spirits. Sunil felt repelled at the sight. The people were steeped in savage ignorance.

Suddenly there was loud screaming. It was the young lady Sunil had seen. She was struggling and people had gathered around her. Sunil pushed his way through the crowd.

'Let me help her!' he shouted. 'I am a doctor.' But he was firmly held back.

'I don't need a Daktar from the city to attend to my daughter,' a man said. 'Leave her alone'.

'But don't you see her condition,' Sunil pleaded, 'you must let me help her.'

'Don't worry about her young man,' a woman chuckled. 'What do you know about maternity? Leave it to us women.' She was one of the village midwives.

Sunil was pushed away. He felt a deep wound in his heart. These quacks and midwives and Yellamma. He must fight them all, he decided. As he walked down the steps, he felt maddened by the deafening noise, 'Udhoh . . .Udhoh

. . .Udh . . .oh . . .oh . . .' He felt as though he had come to fight an impos- sible battle.

Sunil could hardly sleep that night. The memory of the suffering young woman haunted him. He walked into the night, miserable and lonely. In the far distance, he could see the dark silhouette of Yellamma Gudda with a single bright light on the temple tower. There was nobody around and the silence seemed to mock at him.

The next day Sunil could not prevent himself from looking for the house of the young woman. When he found it at last, he saw the father seated at the doorstep.

'Oh, the Daaktar,' he said, 'come in'. 'How is she?' Sunil asked hesitantly.

'Who, Anasuya? Well she had a difficult night but she's alright now. Goddess Yellamma never fails us.'

'Did she go into delivery?'

'The midwife says it will take some more days, but won't you sit down?

Have some buttermilk. Anasuya', he shouted, 'bring us some buttermilk.'

Sunil felt an immediate urge to stop him from troubling Anasuya but the father would not stop talking.

'She came from her husband's home last month,' he said, 'she has no mother and is a bit overworked here.'

Anasuya came with the buttermilk. Sunil was shocked to see her precarious condition.

'She needs immediate medical attention,' he pleaded. 'Please try to under- stand!'

Venkattappa, the father, refused to hear him.

Days plodded on. It was Poornima, a day of special festivity. Yellamma was to be grandly propitiated on that day. As Sunil watched the crowds going up the hill, he felt particularly conscious of the fact that here in this strange, backward village, he was a total outcaste. The Government Dispensary only answered an official requirement. The village quacks and midwives dominated the medical scene with their hideous oils and powders. He wondered whether his existence here was necessary at all.

Dejected, he was walking back to his lodging when he noticed a sudden commotion. There was some stir in Venkattappa's house. There were screams of pain. Anasuya must have entered into labour he thought. People were rushing in and out. The midwife had arrived. All of a sudden Venkattappa emerged from his house. He looked anxious and worried. He was looking for someone.

When he saw Sunil, he ran to him crying, breathlessly, 'Daaktar, she . . . the midwife says it can't be done . . . Anasuya is dying, you must come'.

Sunil rushed into the house. Looking at Anasuya, he knew instantly that this would mean surgery, difficult surgery in fact. Sunil asked for Rajan to be called immediately. When Rajan arrived, he instructed him to bring the surgical requirements immediately.'Don't accept the responsibility sir, 'Rajan pleaded. 'The villagers will not spare us if something goes wrong.' Sunil commanded him to obey. 'Do as you're told.'he said.

Venkatappa trembled and wept.

'You must save her', he cried, holding his hands in his own. With a reas- suring pat on his shoulder, Sunil said, 'Go, Venkatappa, go and pray to Yellamma. I will do my best here.'

As Sunil prepared for the operation, he heard the loud bells of the temple and the anxious supplication of Venkatappa crying out 'Udhoh . . .'

Sunil felt a surging confidence in his heart. He worked with dizzy hope, the sound of the bells lending courage to his heart and dexterity to his fingers. He lifted the baby out at last. It was alive! With tremendous joy, he saw that the danger had passed. The operation had been a success.

It was again a day of festivities. Not Poornima, this time, but festivities to mark the birth of Anasuya's baby. In excitement, the villagers carried Sunil on their shoulders and shouted to the Mother's glory and his as they took him

to the temple. The bells rang again and Sunil felt the divine engulfing his heart. He looked at the Goddess and her gift-bestowing mudras. He knew that by incalculable measure, Yellamma had been responsible for the safe birth of Anasuya's baby. It was indeed She who had made him keep track of Anasuya's condition right from the first day. This was Her way of accepting him and showing the way to win the trust of the villagers. Time and circumstance had brought Sunil and the villagers together. He felt blessed to be able to see a life in the stone image of the Goddess. Here, in this backward village of Yellapura, he had discovered the life that governed every human machine. With fervent joy, he joined in the cry of the villagers. 'Udhoh, Udho . . . Udh . . . Oh . . . oh'

BLOOD CANNOT LIE

Feroze was stunned. The news that the little boy brought had blasted his world. 'Are you sure?' he shouted hysterically.

'Yes, Chacha. People are rushing to the bank building.' 'But who told you?'

'Actually it was the police sirens. I heard them and came out of our house. I followed the police vans and then I heard the whole thing. Shivanna, the watchman is killed. They say the bank has been robbed. People are in a panic.'

The boy continued talking as Feroze hurried to wear his cap and coat. 'But Ibrahim was with him last night. Did you see him there?'

The little boy stared blankly at Feroze.

'Your son Ibrahim, Chacha? I didn't see him anywhere. The police are not allowing anyone near the building. They are using *lathis* to keep people away.' 'Ah, an old man like me,

what will they beat me up for ?Ibrahim can't look after himself. Allah you are my only strength,' he said, looking up towards the
skies.

In a rush he stepped out of his home and walked with hurried strides down the lane. Shivanna was dear to him. He was like his own son. The little boy said he was murdered but what about Ibrahim? He was an idiot boy, unable to manage anything on his own. He had been with Shivanna at the bank the previous night and he was sure of it. Shivanna was his only friend, his only support. He often took Ibrahim to the bank to keep him company during his
night-watch. And now Shivanna was dead. Had Ibrahim witnessed the murder? The horror would have terrified him. He would not have been able to bear it. Feroze's mind was torn between shock and anxiety. When he eventually reached the bank, he tried to push his way through the thick crowd. He shouted to the police officer nearby.

'I must go inside ,' he cried. 'My son is surely inside. He went in with Shivanna yesterday. He's a mentally challenged boy Sir, let me in---I must find my son.'

The police officer patted Feroze on his back and asked him to relate the happenings of the previous night. As Feroze spoke , the officer was touched by his honesty.

'I'm sure nobody's inside, but you can go in and look for him yourself,' he said and sent a constable to escort Feroze.

'He is anxious and in pain,' he told the constable. 'Take care of him.'

The bank looked grim with the smell of death. Feroze blindly followed the constable to the place where Shivanna lay dead. The body was disfigured beyond recognition. Feroze felt weak with sorrow. He wept over the body. The watchman's uniform still clung to his body.

'Why did Allah will it this way,' he cried, 'such a noble soul, killed and burnt like this. Most unjust . . . such a noble soul, such succour to his son, killed and burnt.'

The room was still filled with fumes. Feroze strained his tear-filled eyes in his search for his son. An empty kerosene tin lay discarded at the far end of the room. His son was nowhere to be seen.

'What am I to do?' he wept, 'He must have run out of fear. Where will I find him?'

The constable gently led him away to the officer. 'Did you know Shivanna closely?' the officer asked.

'I've known him since he was a little boy. He spent most of his free time in our house. In fact, last evening he came home to take my son---'

'Take him to the police station,' the officer said. 'We need to interrogate him.'

At the police station, Feroze was questioned and cross-questioned about his acquaintance with Shivanna.

'Oh he was like my own son. He was always there to solve my problems,

a god-sent support, especially with regard to my son, Ibrahim. My son is an idiot and Shivanna cared for him even more than I did. He cared so much that he got him a job at a tailor's shop that paid him for sewing button holes. He never lost his temper with him.'

Feroze broke down and wept uncontrollably.

'He visited us every day without fail, ' he said. 'He couldn't stay without meeting Ibrahim.'

'When did you last see him?'

'Last evening, Sir. Last evening he came home. I was doing my *namaz*. It must have been around six. He said he wanted to take Ibrahim to the bank to spend the night with him.

'Of course, of course,' I said, 'but why don't you wait till dinner? My wife has begun cooking.' But he wouldn't hear. He said that he needed to be at the bank early and that he would buy *idlis* for dinner from the push-cart fellow in front of the bank. He had a kit-bag with him and I asked him if he was travelling but he did not answer clearly. He didn't look himself. I even asked him what was bothering him. ''Oh it's the bank duty," he said, "I have so much to manage all alone. And to top it all, the bank manager leaves the strong room key in the drawer of the table I sit at. The responsibility of the whole bank is on me. It's not that I would steal any of the gold or money deposited there but think of the consequences if the bank got looted? I couldn't bear to see the poor villagers cry over the loss of their savings. Just yesterday, that widow, Thayamma deposited all her gold and land papers to get a loan for her son's college fees. There are countless people like her who come to the bank with so much hope and trust . . ."

Feroze stopped to wipe his tears and clear his choked voice. 'He was an extremely tender-hearted fellow, kind to the poor and ready to help. To the bank's customers, he was synonymous with the bank itself.'

'But what happened later? Did he wait for dinner?'

'No, Sir. He insisted on rushing away. Sir, but what about my son? He's nowhere around. I'm quite anxious, Sir. He tends to lose his way and wanders far if there is nobody to guide him. Shivanna always helped me find him. I am worried, Sir, I don't know what to do.'

Feroze broke down in tears again .Comforting him, the officer assured him of help.

'But I have to carry Shivanna's body to the cremation ground. Please allow me Sir, that would be my last duty to him.'

'It will take a long time. We'll have to wait for the post-mortem. Do you want to wait at home till the body is brought?'

'No Sir, I will go back to the bank. I will wait there.'

Feroze was driven to the bank. He was so weak and shattered that it made the police feel that he was safer inside the building and so was allowed to remain in the bank office. Feroze looked around, hoping to find his son there. The very building that had held out promise to the poor appeared to be a monster, a monster that had devoured the noble Shivanna. He sat on his hunches in a corner of the room. His face buried between his knees, he wept silently.

It was hours before Shivanna's body was brought for cremation. Feroze bought a few rupees worth of flowers to spread over the body. He carried the corpse alongside Shivanna's father.

Weeks passed. Feroze's endless search for Ibrahim turned futile. The police could not catch Shivanna's murderer. One afternoon, Feroze was offering his *namaz* when he heard a firm knock on the door. It was the police. Ibrahim wasn't with them, which meant that they had not yet found him.

'*Salaam Saab*,' Feroze said as he spread the mat on the floor. I would have come to the police station myself.' And then, eagerly, as a thought struck him, 'Have you found the murderer, Sir?'

The police inspector looked grim. He seemed to be struggling for words. 'Feroze, there is some very sad news . . . '

'What is it sir?'

You must be prepared for the worst.'

Feroze stared at him. Minutes passed before he spoke. 'Your son is dead,' the inspector said.

'Huh? How?' Feroze cried out loud. 'Shivanna . . . Shivanna killed him . . .' 'Sir . . . ?'

'Sit down Feroze. Let me tell you what happened. Calm down Feroze. You must be brave. It's very, very disturbing news. Now listen to me and stop being so terrified. Remember you told us Shivanna came here before he went to the bank that night? Well, he took your son Ibrahim with him as you know.

He bought toddy from the liquor shop and plenty of *idlis*-- the pushcart fellow confirmed this. It also showed in the postmortem. He then doused Ibrahim in the toddy, gave him plenty to eat and strangled him, perhaps in his sleep.' 'Strangled him? O Sir! My poor son! I sent him to his death,' cried Feroze between sobs. 'I told him to go . . . I cannot believe this . . . I am a sinner . . .'

'Shivanna is the sinner, Feroze. He was a terrible criminal indeed. He made you trust him. You trusted him but all the time his mind was weaving machinations to loot the bank. He used you and your son to present an ideal picture of his character and to mislead everyone about his identity as the murderer. He made Ibrahim trust him and then killed him.'

'But I still don't understand. How we were mistaken about the whole thing?' 'He killed Ibrahim and clothed him in his watchman's clothes. He was the same size as Ibrahim, you see that helped him. He would have even planned it that way knowing that it was easy to have Ibrahim obey him. He then burnt the body, specially disfiguring the face. He made us believe that he was dead

when in actuality he was the murderer himself. An ingenious plan, Feroze.' A bewildered Feroze asked, 'The body I carried that day, whose was it?' 'It was your own son's,' replied the choked officer. 'You did justice to him--in

his death.'

GIVING UP

Don't we know how our son is torn between us: we his parents and his own family? We know he loves us abundantly and cannot compare it to his love for his wife and his son. And yet, why should he? We are flowers that will fade out soon; his family is what he needs to grow and flourish into a full- grown tree. 'Forget us, son, our days are done,' we tell him but he will not hear. Though we try our best to keep to ourselves, neither interfering nor imposing ourselves on them, my daughter-in-law seems like she cannot accept us as her own. The alien blood in her revolts against us and all her wit and will are used to keep even her infant son away from us.

'Mama, see how he smiles . . . how bright his face is,' my son said, as he put his baby on my lap one day. He knelt down to share the baby's innocent laughter with us. His wife was in her bath and he had taken the opportunity to bring the baby out to us. We felt the baby's soft cheeks and gave him our fingers to hold.

My husband clicked his fingers and made all the bubbly noises he had made to our own son as an infant. I felt a flush of happiness surging within me and bent down to touch the baby's forehead with my own when Kirthi, my daughter-in-law came.

'Who asked you to bring the baby out?' she shouted at my son. 'He needs to sleep after his feed.'

Her rudeness shocked us. The baby was lifted from my lap and taken into

their room. As the door shut behind them, my son tried to smile and hide the shock and pain the incident had created.

'I didn't know it was the baby's sleeping time,' he said while I tried on my part to hide the sadness.

'It's true,' I said, 'babies need to sleep after their feed. Little babies are very sensitive.'

'Is lunch ready?' my husband was asking. I knew from his tone that the question was mainly meant to change the course of conversation. 'I need to be at the auditor's by twelve.' Though the pattern of action was different and innovative each time, Kirthi's object remained the same. We were not to participate in the child's upbringing.

'It's OK.' my husband explained to me. 'It's just that she loves the child so much.'

'It's OK,' I also repeated to myself. 'She has a right to choose how the child should be brought up.'

I for one would never allow myself to trespass into the sweet, young world of my son. The pleasure of watching the grandchild grow compensated for everything. And, for all that, my daughter-in-law did such a perfect job of rearing the child. We admired her strict dedication even as she sternly instructed our son regarding the care of the baby. Things had to change with generations. Our son, however, was not in the least convinced by our arguments.

'The child needs your warmth' he said and 'who could be more loving than you? She doesn't understand your value.'

The problem grew bigger as days went by. At gatherings, however, the embarrassment was an added pain. The child never reciprocated our gestures of love. It was always a huff and a protest against us. Often, we were stared at, as if we were indifferent grandparents who had failed to win over the child's affection. On all these occasions, there always was a tinge of sadness in our son's eyes.

'Maybe we should have continued living on our own,' my husband said, 'it was a weak moment that made us agree to our son's invitation to move in here.'

One night, we heard a loud argument between the couple.

'They are not my parents,' my daughter-in law was saying, 'and I cannot give my baby to anyone and everyone!'

'What about the ayah? Is she not anyone and everyone?'

'But that's my wish. I am the one to choose who cares for my baby.'

My husband and I exchanged a knowing glance. It was time to take a decision.

'The auditor says everything is ready,', my husband said. 'We can leave tomorrow.'

It was a sad decision but necessary for our son's happiness.

We left home during the hours of our morning walk. Our son would be asleep and would suspect nothing for a few hours at least. The taxi had been called and we quietly left with the barest necessities packed in our suitcases. Our intention was to gain as much time as we could before our son found out about us. He would never let us go if he knew of our decision. And the secret would be out had we tried to take all our belongings. We were to enter the old age home arranged by our auditor. My husband had made the required payment. It was a home which would care for us and allow us to work on chores to finance our needs, a haven that offered for a frictionless world of dignity. My husband was given the job of accounting the financial transactions of the home; I opted to assist the head of the home in the household chores. There was no ignominy attached to the job as I was treated with friendship and dignity. I helped in the kitchen and the dusting in the rooms. The lady of the house and I got along well but never spoke about our families.

'I really wish I could have some more sarees,' I told her one day, 'and my husband needs some clothes.'

'I'll be sure to keep it in mind when the next package from the city arrives,' she said. 'We get really good stuff sometimes. Not necessarily old but just discarded . Only, you'll have to pay a small amount.'

That soothed my ego: indeed my husband and I were not yet to be treated either as outcastes or destitute. We had chosen this home for convenience and left our property for our son who was not to be told about our whereabouts. This was the arrangement with our auditor.

One afternoon, the lady of the house called out to me. She was excited and there was an urgency inher tone. She had received the 'right' things for us. My husband and I waited for her to show us the stuff. She pulled out a yellow saree with a green border from the box. And then a purple one -- they looked so familiar!

Wasn't the shawl familiar too? I dug into the box unable
    to control myself.

My husband also had started examining the clothes meant for him. The coat he held in his hand was a birthday gift from me .There was absolutely no doubt. The parcel contained our own clothes left behind in our son's home.

RANGI

If our window had not faced their kitchen window so directly, I would, perhaps, never have known so much about Rangi and that fiendish woman next door. Besides, mine is an old heart, nourished in the rustic warmth of the village where walls are no barrier and secrets never guarded. Though it has been years since we, my husband and I, have come to live with our son in the city, tell me, how could I have shut my ears and eyes when I heard that child shriek with pain, hardly a few feet away? Had I not known the gentle throb of a child's heart? And yet my son always said, 'Don't look into their kitchen, mother, it's not our business.

Whose business was it going to be then? Don't you remember, my son, how it used to be when you were a little boy in the village: in our dear village with its mudwalled house floored with cowdung? When you were a child, my son, every boy in the village was a son of the village, childbirth in another's home was like childbirth in our own. I have nursed so many children and so many others have nursed mine. And my son, don't you remember how the granny of the big house called out to you and your friends in the hot after- noons to give each one a tumbler of freshly churned buttermilk? And don't you remember how she dropped a lump of butter into your tumbler on the sly because you were her favourite? And yet here I am being told not to see and not to hear happenings, so ghastly and cruel. What concrete rules of the city are these? I cannot understand it. Each one's life is one's own--unfeeling

and selfish. I cannot take my mind off Rangi, torn away from her mother so early, sold to work for our neighbours.

Imagine, a nine-year-old, a servant to an unfeeling woman, her husband, her twelve-year-old son and their dog. You can tell from Rangi's face that even the dog is better fed than she is and yet, for belly's sake, she was sold to these people--for a paltry sum of Rs.500.00 a month--all the way from Biligiri Ranga Hills. My son said it was over 300 kms from our city. Rama, Rama, what had the world come to? We also had poor children to help us in the village but we looked after them as our own children and the girl we had was suitably married at our expense. Rangi, poor girl, stopped at our door sometimes and I gave her something to eat but that lady, my neighbour Seshappa's wife, must have espied her at our door and must have threatened her for she suddenly gave up her acquaintance with me and refused even to smile at me when she passed by our house.

'Don't interfere,' my husband said, attributing my feelings to the inquisi- tiveness of an idle prying mind. 'You can never say how these city folk could tarnish our son's name.'

And yet – every day, when I combed my hair and put my bindi in the reflection of the mirror that faced the neighbour's window, my eyes wandered to their house. When I heard Rangi cry, I hurried to the window, bearing the gentle admonition of my husband.

One night, I was dozing off to sleep. We are early sleepers, my husband and I, and we had switched off the light in our room. Suddenly, I was awak- ened by the wailing and shouting next door.

'Amma . . . don't . . . Amma . . . I will not do it again.'

'You beast, you wretch, to have spilt all the milk . . .' Sheshanna's wife was storming at Rangi.

'What is it, mother?' This last voice belonged to her son who had walked in to see what the matter was.

'This beast, look at her, she has dropped the milk vessel . . . the devil.'

Ghastly beatings followed. Since the light in our room was switched off and their kitchen was lit, the whole episode presented itself with the clarity of a movie before my eyes. My heart tore across the strong walls to little Rangi. I saw that lady lean forward to heat the iron spatula over the gas flame; she lunged forwards and I watched, hardly able to move, as she sunk it deep on

Rangi's palms and calf muscles. I felt numb; how could she be so brutal? 'This is what you deserve, you devil,' she cried as she and her son violently

held the little girl's body . . . and God . . . how my heart writhed in pain to see it, the woman pierced her palms and thighs again and again with the hot iron.

Rangi's voice went dry with the screaming. The son watched; he appeared to be enjoying it, was almost gleeful. Suddenly he ran out and brought something--a new instrument of torture.

'What is it, Baloo?' his mother asked.

'A needle', he replied with merciless cunning. 'Watch how I'll poke her body . . .' And he poked the helpless girl with the needle, enjoying her cries of pain.

My husband had woken up and was standing beside me. Casting away all his professed rules of social propriety, he watched this hideous drama with me.

'Can this be, Savithri?', he said, in a tear-filled voice.

The woman dragged Rangi out of the kitchen. We heard the slamming of a door and her shouting, 'Stay there . . . and starve till you're dead.'

My husband and I did not sleep that night. Reminiscences of our old village world and the torment we had witnessed washed out our sleep. In our village home, we may have had only *ragi* and *ganji* to live on, but no one was left unfed in the household. Torturing an innocent child with hunger was a sin, it was unthinkable. Just what was it that made us strangers in the modern world? Was there a new code and an old code for humanity?

Till noon there was no sign of Rangi. After our lunch, we settled down to crushing betel nut and leaves.

In our village home, crushing and sharing of betel was a sacramental matrimonial observance. Throughout our married years, we had enjoyed this tradition and that afternoon, the sharing gave particular comfort to our troubled minds.

The afternoon warmth lulled my husband to sleep and I must have dozed off too for it was with a start that I woke up to the noise on the street. The premonition that it was something to do with Rangi made me rush to the doorstep. A crowd had gathered around the public tap. The heat made me dizzy as I hurried with faltering steps towards the crowd.

Someone said, 'It's the servant girl from your neighbour's house . . . '

Rangi lay at the tap unconscious. Her legs and palms were burnt. The raw flesh burst out from beneath. Her face had shrunk with pain and hunger and shock. Though her eyes were shut, it looked like her whole being was crying with pain. She must have stopped at the tap in a desperate attempt to satisfy her thirst and perhaps her hunger also.

'Why don't we move her to a dry place…?' I said.

No one answered. The look on the faces in the crowd showed that they were in no mood to help. They said it was a 'Police Case' and warned me of danger even if I merely touched her. My emotions welled up in a trice. In anger and in tears, I blurted out the facts of Rangi's condition. They sympa- thised but they were not willing to help her. Such indifference, even in the face, of, perhaps, death?

'How are we responsible?' they asked. 'It is for the law to handle the matter.' I felt alone and helpless, unable even to lift up the fallen child. But, whether in the city or the village, divine succour infiltrates everywhere. Divine succour. Yes, it was indeed that for how else can I explain the sudden appear-

ance of Ganesh, an auto driver and his willingness to help Rangi?

He took Rangi to the government hospital. He even promised to bring me news of her. That night, when Ganesh came back, my husband, my son and he spoke in hushed voices for quite some time. Since I had been told that Rangi was out of danger, I preferred to be alone in my room, exhausted as I already was.

Events passed quickly after that day. Inhibitions of a lifetime were thrown aside in my concern for Rangi, and I agreed to appear before the police to relate Rangi's story. In inscrutable detail, I spoke about the happenings of that horrid night. I related, also, past instances of cruelty as I had known but the police dismissed my story as imagination. They flung aspersions on me as an ignorant woman, incapable of judgement. They avowed that I must have made this complaint to the police to wreak vengeance on a neighbour with whom, perhaps, I had had a quarrel? When my son protested against these accusations, they asked him if he was witness to anything at all? If not, he had no say in the matter whatsoever. They declared that according to police reports, Rangi had never been unkindly treated, that the burns and injuries were due to her accidental fall over a hot pressure cooker and that she was indeed no servant

at all but a poor relative whom Sheshappa and his wife looked after 'out of pity'.

The police seemed to be in a hurry to declare Sheshappa and his wife innocent. My son was convinced that Sheshappa's wife could still be arrested if Rangi's own father would contradict the police reports. He promised finan- cial support to fight the case in court. He contacted Rangi's father and elabo- rated the incident to him. On my part, however, I was concerned only about Rangi and her return to her father.

A few days later, Rangi's father arrived. He was a personification of the poverty which had forced him to barter away his daughter for an insignificant sum. His anguish and despair when he saw Rangi was heart-rending. *What a curse to be a parent in this position*, I thought, when I saw him weep in unabated sorrow.

Like a seedling struggling for life, Rangi's face sprouted in happiness after her father's arrival. Unspoken love showed itself in touching scenes of emotion and, time and again, Rangi said, 'Appa, I want to come home with you. Take me back home with you . . . you will, won't you?'

And Byrappa, the father, replied, sometimes in monosyllables and sometimes with a nod but never with the firmness needed to create confidence in the child's mind.

The next day, talking to us outside Rangi's room, Byrappa poured out his tale of misery. He worked in the Biligiri Ranga temple on a meagre salary of five hundred rupees a month. The marriage of his two sisters had been his burden and he had aged parents to look after besides his own family of eight. During the temple festival, he earned extra money by carrying pilgrims in the 'dholi' up the hills and in the rainy season, when there were no pilgrims, he wove baskets and mats at home. Utter poverty had made him place Rangi and her two sisters to work in families. 'And now, the child asks me to take her back . . . how can I when I can't assure her of even a morsel of food?'

'Then what do you propose to do?'

'I'll have to beg Sheshappa to forgive the child and take here back into his home.'

His answer stunned us. Was this resignation or a determined will to live, I wondered. It looked like the half swallowed rat was destined to return to the ratsnake, after all. Byrappa's face showed the deepest, paternal pain as he said, 'We cannot afford to pamper ourselves with emotions . . . a morsel somewhere is all we can hope for.'

I thought that no father would barter away his daughter if he could help it. 'Byrappa,' my son said, 'I'll pay the same amount as Sheshappa . . . and something more besides, if you'll take Rangi back with you.'

It took some time for Byrappa to understand what was said. Then, as he did, I saw the soft surge of happiness that comes from unfettered love. And, in my son's face, I saw the fulfillment that comes from benediction. In both I saw the flame of humanity that keeps life going and an inexplicable peace pervaded my soul. I folded my hands offering joyous thanks to God.

RINA'S DOLLS

Every evening ,the gentle rap was sure to come. Rina,the little girl from a few houses away, came unfailingly to Lalitha's home to play with the dancing dolls. The rap on the door was like the tremulations of a nervous heartbeat, excited and persisting and when the door was opened, she walked quickly past to the brightly coloured dolls. She perched herself on the stool before the table that held the dolls, smiling with a familiarity and warmth that seemed to say, 'See, I've come . . .'

She engaged in a silent language with the dolls which had now come to be known as 'Rina's Dolls'. Nobody in Lalitha's family really cared for the dolls which were displayed more as showpieces in the front room of the house. Lalitha noticed the sparkle of glee in Rina's eyes as she gently pushed the dancing dolls with her forefinger and watched them shake their necks waists and hands. The sound of her laughter and dance of the dolls vibrated in happy unison. It was hard to believe that Rina could burst out in such exuberant companionship with the mute clay dolls for, at all other times, she seemed to be a shy child more given to silence than the common chattering of little children. Little did Lalitha know that a scared silence was a marked feature of Rina's innate personality. Only the dance of the dolls lured her to laughter. One morning at the breakfast table, Rina's mother announced that they would have guests for lunch. Her face was beaming with brightness. 'Janaki

and Leela . . . you remember Janaki and Leela-- our neighbours in Whitefield? Well, they are coming to see our Sriju. They'll be here in an hour's time --and Rina--you needn't come out to meet them. You could be with your books.'

Rina's big round eyes welled up with tears.

'It's O.K. Rina,' her father said putting his arms round her. 'What would you do with grown-ups anyway?'

Did he expect her to be comforted by his words? Rina was aware that Sriju, her little sister was a lovely little baby and her parents loved to show her off. Withdrawing into her room, she dreamily rummaged among her books turning the pages listlessly, staring at the colourful pictures, imagining how it would be to belong to the world of fairy tales. Could children really be loved and smiled at so? Their dresses were so beautiful and their mothers so different. She could now hear voices out in the sitting room. The guests must have arrived. She hid behind the half-closed door and peeped out. The loud *oohs* and *aahs* coupled with exclamations like, 'How very sweet', 'A perfect baby' and the like made it look like another fairy tale world to her. Anyway she did not belong to it. She strayed away to the window sill where it was her habit to stand and watch the happenings on the road.

Theirs was a quiet, isolated locality with not many vehicles speeding by. Hawkers and passers-by occupied the road-scene and Rina watched them while she drew patterns with her toe. Suddenly, her eyes focused on one lone figure, at the far end of the road. Was it or wasn't it? Oh yes, she clapped joyfully, recogonising her grandfather from the village.

The white dhoti and the black cap--bag in hand--yes, it was him. With a cheerful yell, she jumped down the sill and sped across the living room past the guests, shouting 'Ajja has come'. She ran down the road to meet her grandfather and walked back home holding his hand, laughing and talking excitedly. She walked into the living room, where the guests sat, and settled down on her grandfather's lap smiling happily. But the pleasure did not last long. The conversation soon turned on her.

'Your first daughter is so different—'
'You'll find it difficult to marry her off'

'What with the heavy dowry demands nowadays—' Rina's mother sighed loudly.

'She takes after her father,' she said and her grandfather retorted, 'What

do you say? There's nobody in all our lineage as dark as she is!'

Rina slid down her granfather's lap. Her eyes were filled with tears again. She rushed to her room and closed the door. She stood before the mirror looking at her despised self. She was but six years old but she knew the differ- ence between black and white. She was black and ugly and was not shown off to guests like her sister was. She was never cuddled and did not seemed to be loved as much either. Her little world was a dark world. Only the dancing dolls seemed to welcome her.

It was the annual prize distribution day at school. Rina had been awarded a prize for her essay on 'My Friends.' She had written about the beautiful dancing dolls and the teacher had deemed it 'Very Unusual.' 'A child of deep sensitivity,' she had remarked to another teacher, 'much beyond her age.'

There was great excitement on the prize distribution day. Children were beautifully dressed, happy and smiling with their friends. Rina too had taken the invitation home with the special note requesting her parents to be present on the occasion.

'But I cannot make it from office Rina,' Daddy had said, 'and Mummy will be busy with your little sister.'

Rina had not felt bold enough to insist. One after another, the prize-winners walked up the stage when their names were called out. Rina looked swiftly from the stage to the parents. She noticed their look of pride. When her turn came, a whisper, 'Quick Rina' goaded her on. She did not know if there were any claps for her. She only knew that neither of her parents was present. She held back her tears but she could not stop herself from asking why they had really not come. Again came the agonising refrain, 'It's because I'm black . .

. they are ashamed of me.'

Back at home, Rina gave the prize to her father to unwrap. It was a lovely book full of pictures. Rina' s parents seemed very happy. Rina's clogged soul blossomed for an instant.

'Daddy' she said, hesitantly, 'Daddy I want to buy a doll, please.'

The figures of the Dancing Dolls floated across her mind but no, she would like to have a doll with hair and hands and legs, like Shoba's doll, so that she could dress her up as if it were her own baby.

'Why not. I'll surely buy you one. You deserve it.'

Rina was excited. That night, she slept with a smile on her lips. This was

going to be her first baby doll. She would show it first to Lalita and to the Dancing Dolls.

A few days passed before Rina's father announced that he would take her to buy a doll. Rina rushed to Lalitha's house. Her rap was loud and excited. When Lalita opened the door, she stopped before her and almost shouted, 'Akka, Daddy's taking me today, to buy me a doll!!' There was fresh liveliness in her voice. Lalita hugged to say she was so happy for her. Rina then rushed to the Dancing Dolls pushing them forcefully, swinging her legs and laughing as they shook their heads and skirts to suit the cadence of her own happy heart. They seemed to say they were happy too.

Rina set out that evening dressed in her best. Rina's father drove her to the City Market. Were there shops selling dolls there? Shoba had bought her doll from Commercial Street.

'We must finish fast', Rina's father said as they hurried along the shops. 'Ah, there's a good shop here. Look ---look at this one. Lovely, isn't it? We'll buy this one' and, without paying attention to her mild gesticulations of protest, he bought the doll for her.

Rina felt choked. She burst out in violent tears. The doll bought for her had no legs and hands as she had wished. Its limbs were stuck to the sides of its body, its eyelids were immobile and its face flat and unsmiling. Rina was angry. This was not a doll at all and it could never be her baby doll. When she reached home, she flung the doll onto the floor. She hated it more because it seemed to be like her-- ugly and unwanted. Rina wept while her mother chided her, 'You are never happy with anything!'

For the first time Rina felt that the dancing dolls did not belong to her, that she was alone in her sadness. A chance of a long time had been devoured by the featureless doll. When would it be possible for her to buy a doll again? Why was she not like other children whose fathers would love to hear them ask for dolls. Why was she not beautiful like her sister so that her mother would say, 'Buy her whatever she wants--I hate to see her cry.' Why were her tears considered as nothing? Why did nobody hear her heart's cry to be loved, to be happy?

The next evening, Rina, though ashamed of her tear-ridden face, could not keep away from the Dancing Dolls. Lalitha was not at home and Rina felt relieved. And, the next day, Lalitha never asked her about the doll. This

was why Rina liked Lalitha. She never asked hurting questions. Rina sat before the Dancing Dolls watching their lilting beauty--shaking them again and again repeatedly telling them they were beautiful and lucky to be beautiful.

A few months passed and Daddy planned a holiday to Madras. Rina's baby sister was now over two years and hence considered manageable. The family went about China Bazaar one evening. Rina was fascinated by some colourful, hair clips and broaches. Mother decided they would match her new dress and so they were bought for her. They moved on-- making little purchases here and there, and then, they passed by the doll's shops. Rina's heart beat fast. Would Daddy buy her a doll again?

'No, Rina,' Mummy said, 'remember how you had thrown the doll Daddy bought for you in Mysore! You are not the one to care for beautiful things. Let your sister choose one for herself instead . . .'

Rina watched with eager eyes as her little sister pointed out her choice using vague signs. There was one which Rina especially liked. Just the one she had wished for. She tried her best to coax her sister to reach out for it. Her mother chided her for not allowing the baby to choose for herself. At last, that very doll was bought and her sister was taught to like it and hug it. The doll was not Rina's. Her mother drummed the idea into her head each time she said, 'Now let her alone, Rina, it's her's. Let her play with it.'

Rina believed that sometime, her sister's fatigue or sleep would permit her a chance to carry the baby doll. She would clothe the doll in the set of clothes Lalitha had stitched and she trembled with joy to think how happy Lalitha would to be see the clothes on the doll. She must show the doll to Lalitha. A proper doll at last.

When they reached home, she tried her best to humour her baby sister, but the journey had made the baby irritable and Rina failed in every attempt to take the doll form her. She grew impatient and, forgetting that the doll was not hers, pulled it from her sister's hand. The doll's hand snapped from the elastic and the doll lost its hand before she could even hold it once. Her baby sister yelled and her mother beat her while Rina sadly realised that yet again there was no doll to show Lalitha. Yet again she had no doll she could dress like a baby. Only the dancing dolls remained her own.

SELF DIGNITY

He, Sambashivan, Sam for short had the finest business acumen. Of money and of life. His wife and he had finished all the obligations of their lives: their daughter was married and settled overseas. The daughter's husband was chosen with great care to fulfill the highest parameters of character, upbringing and intelligence. Money, of course, was no concern--he had enough to settle the couple and their children in glorious luxury. And his own son could have nothing to complain about. He had made the same provision for him and his family as well. And for themselves of course. The house they lived in was a miniature palace. The splendour of upkeep and lifestyle was a matter of gossip and discussion. Padma and he had the time of their lives. Nothing stopped them from doing what they had always wanted to do.

'There is that group of small islands that we haven't visited yet,' his wife was saying. 'I wonder if the travel agents have included it . . . ' Padma was looking up destinations on the Internet. 'Such a tiny place and so beautiful . . . the people look like dolls . . . and . . . there's a temple also!'

Sam knew that was going to be their next holiday spot. The travel agent was called in and elaborate arrangements made to practically cover a place of exquisite fancy. Sam loved his wife beyond everything in the world. And she deserved it. It was she who had stood by him during all the travails and turmoils of his life. He had married her at a time when it seemed as though

his life was slipping down a deep abyss, threatening and horrifying. It was she who had worked to support his education and later during his venture to establish what was going to be the first greatest Indian company in the world. When they were to buy the first house of their dreams and were short of finance, she had sold the gold coins she had saved. All along the way, she had helped him to keep up the highest symbols of wealth and wellbeing. Even the bedlinen and towels they used spoke of the finest luxury. They were a couple who knew the value of money and the value of using it right— for themselves and for the evaluation of society. And yet it was not always about the expenses. Perhaps his money-making instincts sharpened over the years. During that time he had shrewdly espied the company, Lifeline which was advertising loudly, calling in quotations for a supply of batteries when they were actually slipping down in the share market. Was this not a strategy to dupe the public? Was this something that could fail to catch his attention? He promptly sent in his quotation, managed to have the order issued in his favour and then, when the company cancelled the order for being on the brink of dissolution, he sued them and bled them dry. Sam had conducted a thor- ough research of deadly diseases and how much was needed to treat a disease. And as always it was their son and his wife who had taught the immediate lesson.

'Blast the insurance companies . . . how do they know what and when something is right for us?' they had argued.

As far as Sam was concerned it was not fifty or sixty or any particular age that signalled a saving plan for himself and his wife. There was the usual look of disapproval on his son's face when he felt that he was spending too much. Too much? Of his money and his own savings?

'Papa do you have to have all those cars lined up? You hardly use them'.

He had the latest models of the most expensive cars in the market. It had been a passion he and Padma had shared – cars and driving.

'What a costly passion!' his son had remarked. 'I'd rather you save for a rainy day' A rainy day? You mean when she or I or both of us would have no money for treatment and you, my son would have to pay? A sneer and a smile had filled his face. Again when Padma was exuberantly volunteering to celebrate the wedding of the maid's daughter, their son and daughter-inlaw had loudly objected. What do they know of the value of money? Sam had asked himself.

'Sixty years ago, your mother and I were married in the Ganapathi Temple. We have still not paid the priest who bought the garlands for us. Could I ever pay him? For that moment and that step in our lives?'

'But Papa, why do you have to do all this? You know money is not an easy thing!'

His son and his daughter-in-law had the same expressions on their faces. The consternation would soon turn to disgust. The disgust would soon turn to open muttering behind their backs and perhaps the grandchildren would follow suit. This had happened too many times of late. They had worn the same scowl on their faces when he had made a large donation to the temple. He had seen it on their faces when Padma had called in the furnishers to change the drapes and the furniture. He had seen the scowl on their faces when Padma bought a new silver dinner set gilded with gold edges.

He had heard the thunder when his son had slammed his room door just because they had couriered a huge box of stuff for their daughter abroad. There was discontent everywhere--

when they changed their mobiles, when they changed their carpets, when they took a holiday . . . and now, the cancer had struck. The doctors had declared that Padma had cancer. Sam decided that she was not to be told about it. She was made to believe that she had a general ailment and was given the best cancer treatment in a general hospital. The doctors, the hospitality, the nurses had all multiplied the scowls.

'Papa, she has to know of it someday. I cannot understand why you waste all that money,' the son said.

Sam smiled. Such remarks, even when it was his own money that he was spending? The bills were mounting.

'You think there'll be any money left?' the son screamed.

Value my son, that's what you yet got to learn, thought Sam. He tore away the calendar sheet on the wall each day and made his entries in the account book. All expenses had been paid by him, including bills like the milkman's. That's how Padma had wished it. The property had been divided wholesomely between the two children. They and the grandchildren would besides be inheritors of his and Padma's names. They would not allow society to sneer at them at any cost.

Padma was drawing her last breath. It would happen any day. He had sent air tickets for his daughter and family. Everything was taken care of. He visited

Padma for two hours in the morning and two hours in the evening. But somehow, on that last day, he came back to the hospital at 10:30 in the night. He wanted to sit with her. He brought the jasmine and the red rose she had always loved. She was in deep coma. He stroked her forehead as he always did. He held her hand and for the first time, the nurse noticed tears in his eyes. She left the room to leave him to his emotions. He left after an hour and returned home. He was tired. But sleep would not come. He swallowed a sleeping pill. The phone rang at 1:45am but was not answered.

He was fast asleep just when they were frantically trying to wake him to give the news that his wife was dead. Griefstricken, the next morning, he slowly walked towards the hospital room. His son and daughter held him. Crowds were gathering.

'Padma' he said as he stroked her forehead again and again. Animal sobs burst out. His body was shaking.

'What time doctor?' he asked. '1:45 am'

'1:45am?'

A gleam of anger crossed his face. *Was it not at 10:30 pm? Was is not when I gave her the rose and wiped her face with my handkerchief?* the words screamed in his head. His son had hired a Maruti Van to carry the body.

'Ah don't I own the best of cars, my son? She gets what she deserves,' he said as he called for the Jaguar which had been her favourite.

He gave his shoulder to carry her royally to the car and to the grave. When he returned to his room, he felt an emptiness he had never felt. He tore off the date sheet from the calendar. He would not have been able to support her for even a single day after that. She had asked him to read her diary after her death. It contained everything she had said. The diary seemed throbbing with life. The incidents and thoughts recorded on all the pages were known to him

– except the last. She had made provision for his life, a long life 'for after this day' she said. 'The lawyer has it all.'

A NEST IN WINTER

Flakes of snow fell like feathers. The last of the flower beds were being covered and it would be months before the daffodils bloomed again. The birds seemed to have left their songs behind, buried in the beautiful white snow.

Amita watched as the cold of the winter took hold of the landscape, rousing memory upon memory, piled one upon the other, thick like the snow. Back in India during this part of the year, the sun would still be shining in mellow warmth but here, in England, it was cold. Amita had come back to England to renew her visa. This was a ritual she had carried out for years. To her it was a renewed pact with Silence. Years ago, thirty five years to be precise, she had entered into a pact with this cold country, when her husband had finally brought her to live with him. This was the land that had promised them everything, a nest of happiness, to protect them against the cold winds of bitterness back in India.

Meeran, her husband had ventured to England to make his fortune. He had been forced to marry before he had found a job and was expected to live on his father's meagre income. His wife, Amita was as beautiful as he was handsome and Meeran had dreams he was determined to fullfil.

'I think, I'll have to go abroad, Amita, to England. They say it's good money over there.'

Amita didn't know how to react. Thirty-five years ago, people in her village

thought of England as an unimaginably far-off land where already married men married again secretly to English girls . . . and . . . she would be left alone in India with her in-laws.

'Don't stop me now. The future will be wonderful, I promise. I will take you to England when I have made enough money,' Meeran had seemed determined and Amita conceded in the end. She forced herself to remain silent on this matter, trusting in her fate and a future in that unknown, distant country. She made her first pact with Silence, even as other people attacked her with their jibes.

'You have no sense,' they said 'letting him go. You think he'll return to you again?'

'It's a clever trick. He'll marry a white woman and settle down. After all, he has no children to return to.'

Her failure to bear children was a constant whip, unleashed on her, by her mother-in-law. 'Four years of marriage and no issue yet? It's a question of the continuation of our family. What about our ancestral tree? The line must continue,' she said. 'and Meeran is our only son. May be he should marry again.'

Amita tried her best to brave the taunts. None had understood the fear and tremor in her heart except her husband.

'You are mine, Amita and only you can be mine,' he once said, quite boldly in everyone's presence. 'Never doubt me.'

His love was both a source of strength and a sorrow to her. Strength because it gave her the will to live; sorrow because such a wonderful love had no lineage.

Amita felt caught in a struggle between life and death. Their economic dependence on her in-laws made life more bitter. Every mouthful of food she ate seemed laden with her mother-in-law's bitterness towards her. And now, with her husband away, she would have to face the situation alone. Her silence, inevitably, grew deeper. She clung to it as if to something sacred, trusting her husband's love for her.

Meeran left for England. He never wrote to her because she was illiterate. He sent her money at odd intervals. He returned to India after seven years, only to go back again. While he was at home, he bought her a small piece of land where she hoped to grow jasmine for profit and to spend her time at

after household chores. A few years later, Meeran returned, this time, to take her with him. He had just a few days to spare and so Amita had to rush through her farewell visits to relatives.

In one of the homes, a daughter of the family had given birth to a deaf and dumb baby boy. The baby was regarded as accursed and only a sense of sadness surrounded the baby's birth. Holding the baby on her lap, Amita saw her own fate in the child's. She herself was endowed with the faculties of speech and hearing, but she could use neither of them if she had to live. The gesticulations of deep pain when the baby cried squeezed her heart. There were only tears, but no sound of crying. Amita lifted up this babe to take home as her own. Meeran agreed and said he would not come in the way of anything that would make her happy. It was a big decision.

'Allah, my God, help me ,' she said. 'Am I doing right? Will I be able to raise this little baby?'

'I will be with you Amita.I will share the responsibility with you. It's a noble decision you have made. Allah is sure to help us.'

Amita felt reassured. She had recognised the magic essence of Life in this creation of God. 'Deaf and Dumb and yet Alive.' she whispered to herself. ' Like me, who must not hear and must not talk and yet be alive.'

She pressed the babe to her bosom with a love that was perhaps greater than the mother's.

It was Life embracing Life. She felt like she had now found a companion in her silent existence.

Amita did not care for the abuses she received from her relatives on her decision to adopt the baby as her own.

'You are only inviting greater sorrow,' they said. 'You can never make anything of this child.'

Amita clung to her decision with determination.

In England, in their little home, the baby had proved to be a true companion and a bright spark of light. Amita felt immense fulfillment when the baby smiled. Meeran named him Surya, the Sun. When they held colourful toys before him, Surya's eyes lit up like sunlight and he threw his hands and legs in joy. Only the sound of laughter was missing. People taunted Amita again, for adopting a child who would never talk, never laugh, nor cry. A doll for all purposes. Only she who had not been able to bear a child could understand the worth of this unwanted sprout of life. It was yet another pact with Silence.

Amita and Meeran were determined to bring sunshine into Surya's life. The society in England was sensitive to Surya's needs and helped him bloom. The school teachers dedicated their best to him and nobody shunned him as useless.

Surya grew up to be a fine, handsome young man. Everyone noticed that he was incredibly smart and intelligent. He grew up to be completely inde- pendent. He found a job in a dance club. He proved to be a wonderful dance teacher. Amita and Meeran were truly proud of him.

Very strangely, that winter afternoon, the sun had shone bright. Surya had come to Amita. His smile was effulgent like the sun. He had seemed eager to tell her something. His face was flushed red as he gesticulated to say he had something important to announce. He was in love!! He had wanted Amita to go with him to the dance school to meet the person he loved! Amita had been excited beyond words. She had felt like a child who was promised a prize. But fear had lurked in her mind. How was she to be sure that Surya had chosen the right girl? How was she to be sure that his love was faithfully reciprocated? If by Allah's grace, Surya had indeed found the right girl, the biggest worry in her mind would melt away like mist! This was surely an incredible ray of hope. She raised a sincere prayer to God to shower His blessings.

The dance club was a short distance away from home. Surya excitedly led Amita to the office and introduced a beautiful young lady to her.

'Do you remember her?' he asked.

The young lady had smiled and said she was Naina, a classmate of Surya's when they were in school.

Oh Naina?!Of course it was Naina, the girl in Surya's class who was particu- larly sensitive to Surya's needs! The girl who was a constant companion to Surya, how could she forget her? She had grown to be a dainty young woman! Her joy had known no bounds when Surya said she was the girl he loved.

Naina had agreed to marry him. This was an incredible benediction from God. The two were wholeheartedly blessed in marriage.

Greater happiness came when Naina gave birth to a beautiful, baby girl. The shrill cry of the baby made Amita and Meeran's joy deeper still. The baby had dispelled every fear from their minds. Amita had succeeded at last in giving a Voice to Silence. In all Amita's pacts with Silence had come her final fulfillment.

After moving back to India, Amita returned time and again to renew her

visa to England. Surya was now a husband and a father but was still her little lamb. Often, she sat watching the snowflakes, with Surya resting his head on her lap. She ran her fingers through his hair vowing never to give him up. In this cold country, she had found a nest in the winter of her life. A nest amidst the snow and songs of joy in the aridity of her heart. An exclamation and fulfilment born of Silence.

PARVATI

In the days when I was a little boy, there was only one hotel in our village, just a sort of zinc sheet shelter with very old benches and tables. The hotel proprietor was also the cook and had only a boy of my age to help him around the place, taking orders, serving, cleaning and collecting money. Now and then, he rushed out to the back of the hotel to draw in a few puffs of *beedi*. We saw the proprietor beat him sometimes for his absence.

There was a large field beside the hotel and here we played *lagori* every evening. The kitchen smells tickled our nostrils and our mouths watered. Long after the game was over, we lingered around, stealthily watching the customers relish the variety of dishes the hotel offered. Food was cooked on firewood and served on aluminium plates. Newspaper cut into squares served as napkins. Used coffee and tea glasses were dipped in a tub of water and wiped dry with a kitchen rag. The hotel used butter liberally on the crisp masala dosas. The *jalebis* and *jamuns* were fried in oil mixed with *ghee*. The smell of spices with all the other smells sparked off a deep yearning for the food in the hotel. And that was the only hotel I saw in all my childhood days.

Today, seated in the manager's chair of the five-star Bonanza, I feel as though I am the king of an empirical domain. Our hotel feels like a dazzling town out from a dream world. Rows and rows of emporia display the most exquisite of goods specially designed to catch the eye of the foreigner. There
are dance halls and restaurants to cater to different tastes. Our staff have been nurtured by me personally in the high refinement required to play hosts to the world's richest customers. Amidst all the grandeur however I feel uncomfortable when I muse on the non-Indian ambience presented by the hotel. The young employees mistake licentiousness for modernity and it disturbs me deeply.For

instance, Rashmi, the girl from my own village flirted so openly with Majnu that her engagement with Murari was called off. And Giridhar from a nearby village cast away his wife and two children to marry Shoba, one of the hotel receptionists. When I tried to intercede, he was so haughty. 'My wife is too old-fashioned,' he said. 'She can't speak English. I'm ashamed of her. I need to keep up standards.'

With the passage of time, I have helplessly watched the crumbling of traditional values among our employees. I have watched with pity the whirlpool of immorality that threatens to engulf them.

The arrival of Parvati as one of our receptionists, however, brought a different colour to the scene. She was one who seemed to have grown into the classicity of her mythological name. She dressed respectably and seemed to honour traditional behaviour. Her long hair was plaited tight and was decked with flowers everyday. Her bindi was always red. Her mangalasutra, with black beads-added dignity to her image. The first time I saw her, I could not help but remembering my mother's shock to see my wife without the mangalasutra.

'What happened Sheela?' she asked anxiously, moving close to her and straining her eyes as if to make sure she wasn't making a mistake. 'Where is your mangalasutra? Did it snap? I'll have it repaired for you.'

'Ah no,' my wife had replied. 'I have put it away on purpose. I can't have it hanging down my neck all the time. It feels like an albatross and gets in the way of the jewellery I wear.'

'Don't say that please,' my mother implored. 'There's nothing more sacred than the mangalasutra for a married woman. Removing it when your husband is alive is sacrilege.'

My wife dismissed her pleas saying, 'I don't need any instructions or advice.

Let me live life as I please.'

The pained look on my mother's face left an indelible mark in my memory. As days went by, I realised how wrong I was in having disregarded my

mother's warning against marrying Sheela.

'She's not the type who'll make you happy, my son. Don't get carried away by the glitter of fashion.'

Now, the image of Parvati seemed to reinforce my mother's judgement. In the first days of her arrival, I realised that Parvati was everything that Sheela was not. She spoke gently and in a dignified manner. She commanded imme- diate respect from everyone in the hotel. My respect for her grew when I saw that she never indulged in any extravagance. I imagined she was keen on saving for her family. I was never close enough to her to understand her family situ- ation but I was sure that the high salary paid by our hotel would end any grinding poverty in her home. I only wished she had the strength to combat the temptations around her. Time proved to me that she had.

'Stay on Parvati,' I heard one of her friends say one day. 'We're having a card party today.'

'Excuse me Riya, but I must rush back home. 'I have to do the cooking.' 'You never spend time with us,' another colleague insisted, but gently and

firmly, Parvati refused to oblige.

My own wife, flippant, quarrelsome and extravagant, drove me more and more to admiring Parvati. Day after day, as I watched her, I felt convinced that an ideal was not unattainable. She was, to me, the lotus that bloomed in ruddy water. When I spoke to my wife about her, she snarled at me and dismissed my description saying, 'Vile creature. She must be a witch. Seducing you men with such impressions.' Such jealousy, such fury! I could never imagine Parvati in like form.

'Aren't we late for the Century Club? Move, you blockhead and get the car out. A nice way to begin the New Year indeed, if we miss the party.'

The Century Club was hosting its New Year Eve party. Down the years the party had acquired fame for its unrivalled grandeur. It was planned impec- cably and offered a surprise event each year. I ,however, regarded it lightly and often chose to be by myself.

'Aren't you getting the car out?' Sheela shouted again. 'You seem determined to spoil the whole thing.'

The hairdresser had done her up with curls this time and I felt like pulling them. The sight of her gaudy lipstick and artificial eyebrows repelled me. She had spent months planning for this night. I definitely would not attend the
party with her. Playing chauffeur to her was shameful enough.

There was an unprecedented rush at the Century. The honking and hooting of cars was deafening. There was a traffic jam and I turned around to shout at the fellow behind me to stop honking---but---it wasn't a fellow. It was a lady and a lady who was familiar to me !

I could not be mistaken anymore. It was Parvati---but, I shockingly observed, a different Parvati altogether. She looked frivolous and liberal. I continued to gaze at her in the rear-view mirror. There was absolutely no doubt. Just what did this mean? My wife thundered at me to move on. I was sweating all over. The car behind me honked again and my hands trembled as I drove on. I never usually planned to accompany my wife to the dance parties but that day, I decided to go in, determined to unravel the mystery of Parvati.

'Are you sure?' my wife asked, 'You aren't dressed for this occasion.'

'I'm not shabbily dressed,' I retorted. 'I'll stay away from you. You won't have to be embarrassed, introducing me to your friends. And there are so many . . .' I didn't need to complete my sentence. Sheela was already way ahead, talking with a friend. As I slammed the car door shut, Parvati's car caught up with mine. She was parking just a few cars away.

'Patsy, Patsy—here,' a voice was shouting. I saw a young man waving out to Parvati. She had alighted from the car. Her hair was not plaited--it was loose and free in the fashion of the day. There was no bindi on her forehead. She was dressed in tight jeans and a sleeveless shirt. When I glimpsed at her after a while, her hand was on the young man's arm. I saw that she wore the most seductive lipstick and enticing colour on her face. She had shunned all her modesty and shyness. I was stunned out of my wits. I was ashamed to have rated her as highly as my mother. *I ought to find out the truth about her*, I told myself and followed the couple, keeping a safe distance to remain unnoticed.

In the fluorescent blue light of the dance hall, it was easier to watch Parvati. I could see her laughing and talking freely, reciprocating the words of love spoken by the young man who was obviously not her husband. I watched her dance after dance, swinging to the western music. My wife was dancing too. I felt impatient to have a closer look at Parvati. There was a lull in the dance sequences and I made haste to find a place very near the dancing couple. At the opportune moment, when her partner was busy elsewhere, I stepped

forward and, trying to sound as casual as possible, said, 'Good evening.'

Parvati's face lit up with recognition as she said, 'Oh, Sir--- how nice to see you!'

'I couldn't tell it was you, Parvati.'

'No sir, not Parvati. Patsy. My name is Patsy.' 'What do you mean? Are you fooling me?'

'No Sir, I'm speaking the truth. I call myself Parvati at the hotel and dress like a traditional Hindu only to keep myself safe.'

'I don't understand.'

'Where is any girl safe nowadays? Men flock around unmarried girls—' 'Unmarried? You're not married? What about your mangalasutra?'

'I only wear it to make people believe I'm married. It's security against men trying to flirt with me.'

I felt my head bursting from all sides. 'But aren't you playing sham?' 'I can't help it, Sir. I have to earn money and keep my chastity as well.'

Patsy introduced the young man as her fiancé. My mind was benumbed with shock and confusion.

It was a cold winter night but I was drenched with sweat. My steps faltered as I walked towards the car after the dance. The window screen was heavy with mist. Lost in thought, I was wiping the screen when I felt a sharp nudge on my side. It was my wife angrily saying, 'Who was that girl you were talking to? Do you know her?'

'I don't know her,' I lied 'She said her name was Patsy. The young man was her fiancé.'

'It looked like you knew her.'

'No. I don't. How would I know her?' I emphasised. Strangely, this time I felt I wasn't lying.

THE CRYSTAL BALL

Supriya felt excited and scared to think that she had fallen in love. She was a little mocking bird hardly on the threshold of womanhood . . . and to think that this should happen to her . . . so suddenly and so wonderfully. She could not believe herself. She bit her finger to make sure she was awake. There was no mistake about it. This was her man.

He arrived every morning at 6.30. He was always dressed in blue and Supriya surmised that he belonged to a factory. First, she heard his cycle bell from a distance and her heart would thump within her like a rolling stone. He stopped, everyday, right before here window . . . only, she was upstairs and he on the wide road with the garden separating them. That was the time when the morning train arrived, and luck had chosen this moment to close the gates on his world and her own, to lock them in a few love-filled moments. Then, the train would pass and he would cycle away. It was a long stretch of hours before she saw him again.

In close proximity to her home, there lived a young fortune-teller, who owned a crystal ball. Her prowess with the conjuring stars was whispered to be stupendous. She, Celine Martis held countless people in stupefaction. Her thin, bony fingers, adorned with gems, were adept at the art of turning the crystal ball. Her small bead-like eyes pierced through starry fortunes with an x-ray sharpness and her voice was onerously shrouded in the mystery of the other world. 'There's no fate I cannot read on the face . . .' she boasted. Her

bright, gaudy clothes and chains of variegated shapes and sizes created a visible flutter in the minds of her customers. She, Celine Martis, however, was proclaimed to possess the most unpredictable temper. On certain rare occa- sions, she was sweet and endearing, speaking to her customers with affection and gentleness but on most other occasions, she was proclaimed to exhibit a shocking feline ferocity. And yet, her unfailing crystal ball and magic charms drew crowds to her door. She was, indeed, the high priestess of fortune, a living Cassandra and, to her ventured Supriya with the secret of her first love. Her tongue stuck in her mouth. She bent her head and fidgeted nervously. Celine's experienced eyes grasped the unquestionable signs. 'Ah', she said, as she turned the ball with an assumed air of serious prediction, 'I see it all . . . I see, it before you can say it.' Expectant and anxious, Supriya lifted up her face. 'Yes, my girl, I see it here. You have a man and you love him,' she said, turning the crystal ball as she spoke. 'But . . . there is a doubt troubling you?' 'Yes', stammered Supriya, 'I love him . . . so much . . . but I don't know . .

. ' 'If he loves you? Well, your stars are bright. Go ahead, my girl. I will give you a charm. Come back tomorrow and tell me .... Supriya felt strength-

ened and happy. Her heart fluttered like a butterfly and her fingers trembled as she placed the money on the table.

Supriya waited at the gate the next morning. She had the charm in her hand. In the distance, appeared her man. The railway gates closed and he halted. She looked at him fully for the first time, from this close a distance. He was bewitchingly handsome. 'He is dipped in beauty,' she told herself and, before she knew, the minutes had run out and he had moved on.

'Try again' Celine told her. 'This time, I will give you a stronger charm'. Supriya had drawn heavily from her bank account and she decided she would ask for a fresh allowance from her father if need be. She paid more than Celine always charged. 'You are sure to get him,' Celine assured. I shall be so grateful', said Supriya.' 'And I shall be the happiest' Celine said.

The next day dawned dark and gloomy. Supriya dragged herself out from her warm bed, excited and nervous as she subjected herself to the rigours of beautification with tremendous zeal for the sake of him she swore she loved but had not the courage to speak to. 'You must make up your mind', Celine had said, 'and,

remember, the charm is very, very powerful '
Minutes slipped

by and Supriya ran across the garden gate. There he was! The railway gates

had closed and he stopped a few feet away from her. Celine's charm must have worked for, how else would one explain the derailment of the goods train and the consequent closure of the gates for an unspecified length of time? Supriya directed her steps closer to him. 'The trains derailed . . .', she said. 'Huh . . . Huh . . . Damn it' he cried as he pulled up his sleeve to look at his watch, 'I will be late!' he said angrily.

'Why don't you come in to our house . . . I live in this house here . . .' said Supriya hesitantly.

'It's alright here, little girl,' he said. 'In the shade of the tree, only, damn it, the thing will take long.' He pulled up his sleeve again to look at is watch. 'Well, have you a telephone in your house? Yes? Well, can I make a phone call? O.K . . . then . . . ' and he turned his bicycle into her compound.

Supriya was floating in happiness. No one in her house was up that early hour and she reigned supreme over the few, blissful moments. 'Please stay . . .' she said, after the call, but he would not hear. 'No, no, I will have to take another route. Thanks, anyway.' and then, he hurried out.

'What did you say your name is? Supriya, isn't it? I'll remember, 'Thank you,' he remarked before leaving.

So handsome and so dignified. Truly, he was the hero of her dream come alive.

Day after day, she waited for him, for those brief moments at the gate while all else in her family slept. Each meeting added to the totality of her triumph in, as she told herself, having surely won him.

Suddenly, one morning, he said he wished to meet her parents. Gosh! Had the big day come at last? She rushed to the priestess of fortune. 'Celine', she shouted, as she entered, 'you have done it at last . . . you are simply great'.

With unabated excitement, she related to her the happenings of every day and, specially, of that day/.

'I am sure he wishes to ask for my hand,' she said, as she emptied her purse on Celine's table. 'It would never, never have happened if you hadn't helped. I have even clicked a photo of his and he signed it for me. Here . . .this is him'

Celine chuckled in glee as she held up the photo to the light. Suddenly, her face turned dark and terrible, her smile hardened and her fist stiffened.

'Who . . . who?' she screamed between her teeth. 'Is this he? And did he

sign it for you? You beast, you wretch . . . so this is what you've been doing eh? Robbing me of my husband? With my own charms?'

Mad with fury, she flung the crystal ball at Supriya and pounced upon her like a wild cat.

CHANDRIKA

No one could have imagined that so many souls breathed in the dance hall that night. Braving the cold winter winds and snow in the city of New York, hundreds had gathered to witness the dance performance of a great dancer of world repute. In the stillness of the hall, the only sounds were the hazy jingle of bells from off-stage and the musicians trying to tune their instruments. The lights came on, slow and dim, creating an austere environment of suspense. Suddenly and dramatically, Chandrika, the dancer, made her appearance. Her expressions and form exhibited an astounding sublimity of human grace. The tabla beat paused in the stillness, the shehnai wooed Time itself and the singer swung Silence into action.

The beautiful damsel began her dance, fervently offering obeisance to the brass image of Nataraja, the Lord of Dance. In graceful gestures, she lit the oil lamps placed before the deity. The soft, alluring music from the instruments and the devotional chanting of praise to Nataraja created a mood of deep veneration, setting the tone for an evening of exquisite art experience. Chandrika prostrated and began her dance, invoking the Lord's blessings and glorifying His greatness. The hushed silence added to the solemnity of the event. In the mystic light of the lamps' flame, it appeared as though the static figure Nataraja would come alive and the two would blend into one through their art.

Chandrika stopped to introduce her first item. The spotlight fell on her beautiful face. She was surely the light of the Moon. Her eyes reflected the

brightness of an ecstatic soul and, when her lips parted, the voice that emanated seemed to be the voice of a veena translated into human tongue. The experi- enced gaze of the dancer trailed from row to row . . . none realising that it was, indeed, a search . . . till, finally, her gaze rested on a gentleman, dressed in an impeccable white kurta and seated at the corner of the second row. He was keenly observing the stage. His face showed signs of delicate emotion. 'Ah! There he is!' Chandrika exclaimed silently. She choked for an instant before quickly gathering her presence of mind. 'The flame is unspent', she said to herself with a mock smile, 'luringly handsome, even now, after so many years. But, alone?' Releasing herself from that gaze, she turned to introduce her first item of the evening. 'The exposition you will now witness is that of the divine couple, Radha and Krishna', she said. 'Radha, the sincere and beautiful one, waiting for her errant Lord all through the night . . . '

The music was painful and languishing. Radha, alone, lovesick, jealous, afraid. 'Who could be the evil one that might have bewitched him? Oh, cursed be the night! May the heat of my anger and the river of my tears stamp out the dark night forever.'

Stealing upon the height of her lamentation, her Lord appeared, nervous and guilt-ridden. Radha cast herself in an unshakeable pose of anger while He, the Lord of the Universe, wooed her gently and patiently.

'Your body smells of jasmine and your lips have been sucked of their colour' she accused him.

'I only stopped to pick some jasmine for your braid of immeasurable beauty,' he said, 'and I tasted the mulberries I plucked before offering them to you.'

'And where are the jasmine? Oh empty-handed One! And where, oh tell me where, are the sweet mulberries you plucked?' The question seemed to challenge the answer given by Krishna. Was it going to be a shameful letdown for the Lord? Radha looked anxious for her Loved One. The audience eagerly awaited the conclusion to the divine sport.

'Alas! With a start I realised I had overrun the time and in haste and confu- sion, I dropped the two, keen on rushing to you.' The Lord Krishna succeeded as always and Radha, the truthful one danced in happy submission to her love. The crowds clapped loud as if celebrating the happy unison.

Chandrika's dance was scheduled for five days, While she replaced other dances with new ones everyday, only the Radha-Krishna dance remained,

enacted with increasing intensity. Day after day she hurled her questions at the Immortal One, her gaze fixed at the figure that sat, sometimes, in the second and sometimes, in the first row.

'You have pained me, Govinda. Tell me, which of my actions has borne this fruit? I worshipped you so truthfully and yet, why did you betray me

?'She had asked the person in the audience this question, years ago in this same city, crying a lament in real life. He had, then too, been a part of the audience and perhaps, drawn by the flashy grandeur of stage beauty, coaxed her into marriage. Beauty at home had not quenched his desire for new pleasures, and he, had wandered off, like a sinful bird in the dark night.

Lying awake in the hotel room that night, her mind travelled back to the time when she was on her first dance performance in New York. She was then at the brink of her teens. Her parents had brought her to dance on an immensely reputable stage. It was then that the man in the audience had come into her life. Exceedingly handsome and soft in demeanour, he had drawn her to love him and she had given herself up to him like Radha to Krishna.

'You will be putting our family to shame,' her mother had argued, 'think of your sisters. We can never get good marriage alliances for them if you marry this man. What do we know of him except that he's an Indian who loves your dance performance?'

'It's not only about caste, Chandrika,' her father had said. 'You are only eighteen and don't know the ways of the world. We know nothing about his family either.'

'No Appa. I can't marry anyone else. I trust him wholly. I won't come back to India with you.'

The parents were aghast.

'You will not come home with us? Do you understand what you're saying?

New York isn't an easy place to live in.'

'I have brains enough to manage my affairs, Amma. I don't need anyone's help.'

Her words had shocked her parents.

She wouldn't allow them to meet Raghava for fear they would draw him away from marrying her.

'We leave you to your fate. We will have nothing to do with you from now,' her father said, after a painfully persistent effort to make her change her

mind. Her mother was in tears when she bid goodbye and said , 'Look after yourself, dear. We leave you against our wish. We have your sisters to care for.' Lying in the hotel room that night, staring wide-eyed at the ceiling, she remembered with remorse the events that followed. She lived in bliss only for a few months after she married Raghava. Beauty at home had not quenched his desire for more and he wandered like a sinful bird in the dark night. Suspicions about his fidelity left her in sheer confusion. She had no friends to confide in. The city of New York, which had seemed heaven to her, now

appeared baffling and her helplessness added to her misery.

'This is how I am,' Raghava retaliated. 'If you aren't happy with me ,you can leave.'

In utter desperation, she telephoned her parents.

'You are no more than a street woman now,' her father shouted, 'you can't expect us take you back and spoil your sisters' lives. Do what you want but keep away from us. I will send you money to return to India if you so wish.' It was then that her dance guru came to her rescue. 'Come, child,' he said. 'Be a daughter in our family. We have no children of our own. God has sent

you in answer to our prayers.'

He gave her shelter and direction to recast her life. He reiterated that her art would never let her down. He prophesied that she would grow in fame and forget the darkness that shrouded her.

'You have pained me, Govinda, tell me, what sin did I commit to deserve this? I worshipped you so truthfully. Tell me why did you betray me?' Shocked, angry and shattered, these are the questions that she had asked him years ago in this very city. Lord Krishna and his many loves are worshipped and praised for He, the immortal One, is in everyone and everyone is in Him. His is the spirit of the Divine. His female devotees, the *gopikas*, symbolise the thirst of the human soul for the Divine. But, when her husband, a human, stooped so low, Chandrika was compelled to turn her face away.

'Will you ever understand the pain of the betrayed?' she asked the Errant One, the question churned from the depths of her heart. The crowds clapped in jubilant applause.

On the fourth day of the performance, Chandrika spotted Raghava seated in the first row. She also spotted the flash of a white handkerchief drawn across his face. He seemed to be wiping his tears. Delight surged in her vengeful

heart. 'Have you no feeling for me?' she had asked years ago and there had been no answer. Neither guilt nor shame, only defiance. And now . . . the white handkerchief . . . but what did it matter to her? She had found her solace and her love in dance. With dizzy fervour, she danced on and on.

'When you close your lips on mine, And hold my hand,
    the moment is not ended.

It passes on to me when I am alone,
Speaking of you and me in symphony.'

On the last day too, crowds thronged in unabated number. After this day, Chandrika was to leave this city yet once again. Her dance amidst living memories would come to a halt.

The curtain opened and the lights came on. Chandrika felt her feet heavy and unwilling. She felt her spirit dissipate, conscious that she would look for him for the last time. He was not there. Her eyes darted from row to row but the hall only screamed his absence. The music started. She danced the Radha- Krishna dance. Again, jealous, afraid, angry and sad, Radha wandered in the empty night. 'Who could be the vile creature who has seduced him away from me? The hour is steeped in darkness and yet he has come not. Oh, will he never understand the pangs of my lamentation?' When Krishna did appear on the stage, she looked expectantly for him who may have entered also but it was not to be. In anger, she refused to accept the cajolings of the Dark one. 'If you shun me now, your loneliness will haunt you and you will long for me when I am gone,' Krishna said as she lifted a hopeful gaze towards the audience once again. Her body was hot with disappointment. She next decided to dance the dance of Shiva Nataraja, the Lord of Dance. That alone would ease her heavy soul. The accompanying music started. The singer sang in a

high emotional pitch,

'The flame of love has burnt. Burst into an orgy of love. Unanswered by Acceptance, Unrecognised.

But, no matter.

The flame has fire to burn itself.

Negativity shall destroy all.

Ashes shall drop, bereft of desire

and Shiva the Lord shall smear His body with them, Answering the unanswered,

Recognising the unrecognised.'

The crowds clapped in thunderous applause. The curtain fell for the last time. Chandrika felt no inclination towards the autograph books. With a soul of lead, she dragged herself away. Her legs were weak and her heart loud. It was a glimmer of hope that had led her to New York again. In the four days of her performance, the glimmer had transformed into bright stars. Though she refused to accept it, she was guilty of an arrogance and a denial of accept- ance when she spotted him in the audience. On the fifth day, the stars vanished. The dance programme , the applause from the audience and the recognition in New York were meant nothing to her. Life itself had lost its meaning. She wished to rest and to be comforted. Tears rushed to her eyes, as she walked slowly with trembling legs towards the green room and there, through the mist of tears, she saw him ,waiting for her!His face was swollen from weeping and he had a sorrowful, pleading look. 'Forgive me Chandrika' he said, 'come back to me, please.'

Chandrika stopped for an instant. She then slid into his arms and rested her head on his shoulder, submerged in an ocean of happiness.

ABOUT THE AUTHOR

Vinoda Revannasiddaiah believes in the power of the writer in translating the finest human emotions and sensibilities into language. Particular situations and the response of individuals to them constitute the crux of her stories. *The Crystal Ball and Other Stories* was previously published under a different title and was NYC Big Book Award 2019 Distinguished Favourite.

www.ingramcontent.com/pod-product-compliance
Lightning Source LLC
LaVergne TN
LVHW061553070526
838199LV00077B/7030